To Izzy, the artist
in our house.
L.K.

For Elsie and all her
fabulous artwork.
J.W.

FABER & FABER has published children's books since 1929. Some of our very first publications included *Old Possum's Book of Practical Cats* by T. S. Eliot starring the now world-famous Macavity, and *The Iron Man* by Ted Hughes. Our catalogue at the time said that 'it is by reading such books that children learn the difference between the shoddy and the genuine'. We still believe in the power of reading to transform children's lives.

First published in the UK in 2020
First published in the US in 2020
by Faber and Faber Limited
Bloomsbury House, 74–77 Great Russell Street, London WC1B 3DA
Text © Lou Kuenzler, 2020 Illustrations © Julia Woolf, 2020
Designed by Faber and Faber
US HB ISBN 978–0–571–35170–1
PB ISBN 978–0–571–35171–8
All rights reserved.
Printed in India
10 9 8 7 6 5 4 3 2 1
The moral rights of Lou Kuenzler and Julia Woolf have been asserted.
A CIP record for this book is available from the British Library.

FSC
www.fsc.org
MIX
Paper from
responsible sources
FSC® C016779

✦ A FABER PICTURE BOOK ✦

Calm Down, Zebra

Lou Kuenzler   Julia Woolf

FABER & FABER

Annie said to the animals, "Let's help baby Joe.
He's learning his colours, which he doesn't yet know.

I'll paint pictures of you – please line up for me.
If I use the right colours then Joe will soon see.

"Frog, fetch the **green** paint.
That's perfect. **Well done!**

And Lion, you're **yellow,**
as bright as the sun.

Next I'll paint Cat,
as **black** as the night.

"But, goodness me, Polar Bear! You don't look . . .

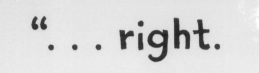

"... right.

"You're supposed to be plain like the ice or the snow.
Those crazy **pink** lines will confuse little Joe."

The sheep and the llamas were all just as bad –
someone had gone completely stripe mad.
"Who did this?" asked Annie.
But it was easy to guess.

Her old stripy friend was behind all the mess.
Joe wriggled and giggled. He clapped with delight.

But Annie said firmly, "**No Joe, it's not right!**
Orangutan's **orange**. She should not be bright **blue**.
Calm down, Zebra. This just will not do!"

But Cheetah had joined in giving everyone spots.

While Lemur did rings . . .

. . . and Dalmatian did dots.

"Behave!" Annie warned. "Please all just calm down.
Do not copy Zebra – he is being a clown."
But then Annie saw there was still worse to come.
Zebra had painted on Elephant's . . .

BUM!

Annie tried to look cross, but she started to laugh.
And she couldn't stop grinning when she spotted Giraffe.

"Peacock!" cried **Annie**, her eyes wide with surprise.

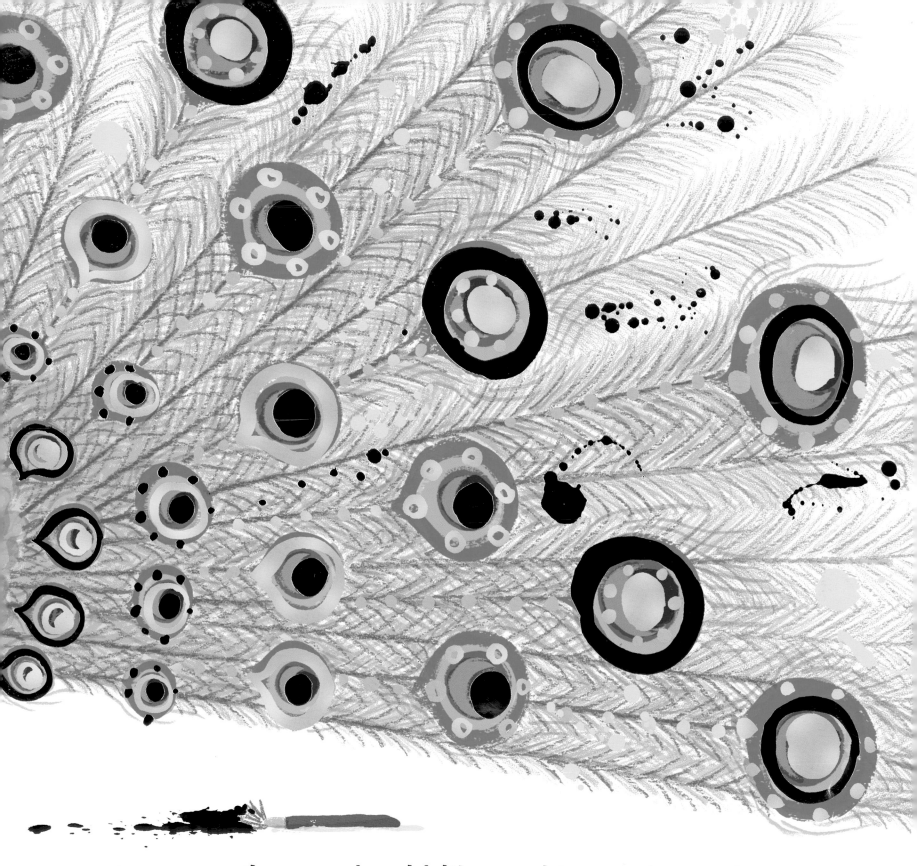

He was silver and gold like a shimmering prize.

Annie looked all around at what Zebra had done.
It was wild and colourful, zany and fun!

"Oh, Zebra!" she cheered.
"You were right from the start.
Joe should choose his own colours.
Let's all make some art."

Annie handed out pictures in plain black and white,

saying, "Colour them in however you . . .

"like!"

Then Joe took a paint pot . . . .
and Zebra did too.

Joe started with **green**,
and Zebra picked **blue**.

They painted each other from their heads to their toes –

two shimmering, glimmering, stripy . . .